PAOLO

EMPEROR OF ROME

AUTHOR
MAC BARNETT

ILLUSTRATOR
CLAIRE KEANE

Abrams Books for Young Readers • New York

Ah, Rome! The eternal city.

A place of fountains, food, and music.

A place of chaos and beauty.

Above all, a place of freedom.

But not for Paolo. Paolo lived confined to a small hair salon on Via Torino. Often he would press his nose against the window, captivated by the bustle on the sidewalks.

"Get away from there, Paolo!"
Signora Pianostrada would shout.
"You're smudging the glass."

All night Paolo dreamed
of the sweet life in Rome,
and all day he did the same.
(There was not much else to do in the salon.)
"Lazy Paolo," said Signora Pianostrada.

Sometimes the signora would open the door to sweep a pile of ladies' hair out onto the street. Paolo would run over, his nails clicking on the tile floor, but the signora would block the exit by simply lifting her foot. On these occasions, Paolo would poke his nose outside and, sniffing, smell all the smells of Rome—salty, sour, meaty, flowery. That was all Paolo got of liberty: a whiff.

Oh! But one glorious day there was a breach!
The widow Garibaldi, arriving for her weekly
appointment, failed to shut the door behind her.

Paolo waited for the mistake to be discovered,
but already the signora was putting curlers in the widow's hair.
Should he? Could he?
He did.

Paolo was free!

And was the city all he imagined? It was more.
Bridges and plazas and tall cathedrals.

Ruined temples

and busy cafés.

And statues! Statues of humans
and gods and horses. Statues of lions that
shot streams of water from their mouths.

And high on a hill, topping a column,
a statue of a proud she-wolf,
the mother of Rome.
"How like this wolf I am," said Paolo.
"But whereas she is made of stone,
I am made of muscles,
and can go wherever I please."
But wherever should he go?

Of course! The Colosseum.

Paolo stood on the ground of the great arena.

Here, thousands of years ago, men and dogs were kept in cages
and forced to fight. "How beautiful to build such a towering marvel,"
said Paolo, "and how cruel to fill it with barbarism."

The little dog's soul swelled up so he thought his ribs would burst.

In the middle of the city, Paolo found
a field full of ruins and lounging cats.
It seemed a good spot for a nap.
But no sooner had Paolo entered
than a huge tabby bounded over
and challenged him.

"What business do you have here, little dog?"
(And it was true: The cat was bigger than Paolo.)
"I am here to have a nap."
"This place is for the cats," said the tabby. "Nap elsewhere."
Paolo puffed out his chest. "I will not."

The cat hissed and swiped her claws. Pain spread across Paolo's face. He had been cut, and deeply. But rather than flee, Paolo stood and barked. The cat, frightened by Paolo's indifference to injury, disappeared into the grass.

Paolo hopped from column to column till he stood upon the tallest.

"I am Paolo," he said. "The biggest among you has scratched my cheek, and I did not flinch. Will any other cat challenge me?"

The cats were cowed.

Paolo curled up and slept.

He was awoken by the sound of swelling music. "I would like to hear more of that," Paolo said. He climbed down the columns and sneaked into the opera house. Around him rose arches as in the great Colosseum, but here people watched while a man sang a sad song.

When the singer finished, the crowd applauded. They shouted, "Bravo!" and threw down roses.

"It must feel wonderful to be adored," said Paolo. "I should like it if one day people shouted for me."

The opera had made Paolo hungry.
He threw himself back into the madness of the city,
wandering down alleys till he found himself eating
from a trash can behind the finest restaurant in Rome.
"Truly," said Paolo, "I am living my life."

But Paolo's supper was interrupted by the sound of snarls.
A pack of ragged curs had crept up behind him!

"This is our street," said their leader, who was called Brutus.

Paolo laughed. "The streets are for everyone."

The dogs considered this.

Brutus asked, "Who are you to say so?"

"I am Paolo, that escaped from his prison and is like the wolf come to life. I have drunk from the mouth of a lion. I have stared down the cats who live in the ruins. And I will lead you, if you like."

The decision was unanimous.

All votes were for Paolo, even from Brutus.

It was unprecedented.

That night, Rome belonged to the dogs.

When the sun rose,
the pack scrounged up a delicious breakfast.
The sun streamed through the buildings
so that the streets appeared pink.
Paolo's heart was at peace.

But what's this commotion? Six nuns had fallen into the Trevi Fountain!
The crowd in the piazza, stupefied, looked on at their awful splashings.
"How terrible!" said Paolo. "We must do something!"
"Of course it is terrible," said the dogs.
"But what concern is it of ours?"
This was outrageous.
If heroism was not
to be found in the pack,
then Paolo must act alone.

He leapt into the water and, careful not to tear their habits,
pulled the nuns to safety, one by one.
The carabinieri, arriving on the scene with several life preservers,
were astonished to find Paolo had done their work for them.

The captain was at first put out, ashamed to be outshined by a small dog.
But the cheers of the crowd were contagious, and soon even the proud officer
joined in. "Bravo, Paolo!" he shouted. "I'll see you receive a medal for valor!"

Paolo got more than a medal.

In the afternoon, he was granted an audience with the pope.

The pope scratched Paolo's ears. "I should make you a saint," he said.

A sour cardinal frowned. "Your Holiness," he whispered,

"it is impossible. He is still living. And besides, he is a dog."

"Surely," said the pope, "we could make an exception . . ."

The cardinal shook his head.

No matter! Paolo was given a fine room in the papal apartments.
Each night the chefs prepared for him some new feast. His bed was
made with satin sheets and piled high with goose-down pillows.
The walls were covered with paintings by the old masters.
Paolo studied the pictures and was impressed by their beauty.

But he preferred to look out his high window, from which he could see all of Rome sprawled out before him. The paintings were lovely, but they did not move. The city was always stirring.

And so after some weeks, Paolo made his decision.
He bid farewell to his grand apartment.
The guards saluted him as he passed
through their gate and into the city.

The little dog trotted down winding streets, his nails clicking on the cobblestones. Back to the tumult! For walls are walls, even when papered in gold and hung with Caravaggios.

And Paolo's proud spirit was boundless.
He could not be contained.

For Nick Villalon
—M.B.

For my brother, Max
—C.K.

The illustrations in this book were made using
Photoshop and Procreate.

Cataloging-in-Publication Data has been applied for and
may be obtained from the Library of Congress.

ISBN 978-1-4197-4109-8

Printed and bound in China

10 9 8 7 6 5 4 3 2 1

ABRAMS The Art of Books
195 Broadway, New York, NY 10007
abramsbooks.com